D1439453

For Finbar

First published 1987 by
Walker Books Ltd
87 Vauxhall Walk, London SE11 5HJ

This edition published 1997

2 4 6 8 10 9 7 5 3

© 1987 Colin and Jacqui Hawkins

Printed in Hong Kong

British Library Cataloguing in Publication Data
A catalogue record for this book is
available from the British Library.

ISBN 0-7445-5230-3

Terrible, Terrible TIGER

Written and illustrated by

Colin and Jacqui Hawkins

FALKIRK COUNCIL
LIBRARY SUPPORT
FOR SCHOOLS

WALKER BOOKS
AND SUBSIDIARIES
LONDON • BOSTON • SYDNEY

There once was a terrible tiger,
so terrible to see.

There once was a terrible tiger,
as fierce as fierce could be.

There once was a terrible tiger
that looked down from a tree.

There once was a terrible tiger
that came creeping after me.

There once was a terrible tiger
with teeth as sharp as sharp could be.

That terrible, terrible tiger –
will he eat **me**?

That terrible, terrible tiger,
he roared ... and leapt at me.

I cuddled that terrible tiger.
He's really my kitten, you see.

FALKIRK COUNCIL
LIBRARY SUPPORT
FOR SCHOOLS